THE RECRUIT

KICK!

THE RECRUIT

K. R. COLEMAN

MINNEAPOLIS

Darby Creek
A division of Lerner Publishing Group, Inc.
241 First Avenue North
Minneapolis, MN 55401 USA

For reading levels and more information, look up this title at www.lernerbooks.com.

The images in this book are used with the permission of: iStockphoto.com/Smileus; iStockphoto.com/Purdue9394; iStockphoto.com/PhonlamaiPhoto; iStock.com/sumnersgraphicsinc.

Main body text set in Janson Text LT Std 12/17.5.
Typeface provided by Adobe Systems.

Library of Congress Cataloging-in-Publication Data

Names: Coleman, K. R., author.
Title: The recruit / K.R. Coleman.
Description: Minneapolis : Darby Creek, [2018] | Series: Kick! | Summary: With her family's farm failing, Tessa's best hope of attending college is a soccer scholarship but the offer her best friend helps arrange would mean giving up her boyfriend.
Identifiers: LCCN 2017029923 | ISBN 9781541500235 (lb : alk. paper) | ISBN 9781541500334 (pb : alk. paper) | ISBN 9781541500341 (eb pdf : alk. paper)
Subjects: | CYAC: College choice—Fiction. | Soccer—Fiction. | Dating (Social customs)—Fiction. | Best friends—Fiction. | Friendship—Fiction. | Farm life—Kansas—Fiction. | Kansas—Fiction.
Classification: LCC PZ7.1.C644 Rec 2018 | DDC [Fic]—dc23

LC record available at https://lccn.loc.gov/2017029923

Manufactured in the United States of America
1-43655-33472-9/29/2017

The book is dedicated to my nieces, Rachel and Riley—two soccer players I adore!

TESSA Dobbs scrubs at her face, trying to keep the rain out of her eyes. It's been raining since halfway into the game. By now, with just two minutes remaining in the second half, the rain is falling hard and fast, biting against Tessa's skin as she moves the soccer ball down the field.

With the score tied at 1–1, Tessa is determined to get in one more shot. These last few games of the season are most important. If the Carlton Colts win enough games, they'll qualify to go on to the quarterfinals, then the semifinals, and then—hopefully—the state championship. Tessa isn't ready for her last season of high school soccer to end just yet. She splashes through a puddle, eyes on the net, as her teammates charge the field behind her.

Ellen, her best friend and one of her teammates, calls that she's open as she sprints down the field. She's by far the fastest girl on their team.

Tessa signals to Ellen. Ellen goes wide, and Tessa makes a quick pass to her. Ellen catches it, turns, and runs down the center of the field. Less than a minute on the clock now. Tessa zigzags across the field, trying to shake the Richfield Wildcat defender who's following her.

The ground is a mess, but Tessa won't give up. Her heart is pounding as she darts away from the defender. They could still win this game—they have the momentum now. This is their chance to beat the Wildcats, who've won every other game against the Colts for the past four years. She's not about to let them win one more.

As soon as Tessa gets open again, Ellen passes back to her, but the rain and wet grass slow the ball. One of the Wildcats runs to intercept it, but Tessa beats her to the ball and takes the shot.

The ball spins and arcs through the falling rain. The Wildcats' goalie leaps up and tries to stop it, but the ball slips past her hands and goes in. The buzzer signaling the end of the game goes off.

Ellen runs toward Tessa, and they leap up and grab each other in a wet, muddy hug. "We did it!" Ellen shouts to Tessa. The rest of their teammates cheer as they join them, circling around the girls until everyone is roped in. Tessa can hear their family members celebrating in the stands. Sports are huge at Carlton High, and home games for any Carlton team draw big crowds. Tessa wishes her parents could have made it to this game. But her mother had to work and her father was still out in the field, racing the storm when she'd left.

That's OK, she reminds herself. *There will be more games.*

Coach Andrea pumps her fist in the air. "Nice job, girls!" she shouts, jogging over to them. She gives Tessa a high five. "That was a beautiful shot, Dobbs."

Tessa grins. "Thanks."

"All right, everyone," Coach Andrea shouts over all of them. "Let's line up and then get out of this rain."

Both teams line up and exchange handshakes. The Wildcats look grim, although Tessa doesn't blame them. The Wildcats have lost enough games this year that they needed to win this one to make it to the quarterfinals. Their season is over. Some of the seniors may go on to play soccer in college, but for many of them, this was their last game outside of rec leagues and pickup games. Her stomach twinges at the thought—she could be in the same position soon.

After they attempt to clean up in the locker room, Ellen and Tessa walk out of the school together. "Oh, my sister made it to the game after all," Ellen says, pointing to a girl standing under a red umbrella. "Come say hi!"

They join Ellen's older sister, Sadie, at the edge of the parking lot.

"Great game, you two," Sadie says. She and Ellen look like they could be twins, even though they're three years apart. It's been a while since Tessa last saw Sadie, but she's still as tall and graceful as ever. Even when standing in a downpour.

"Thanks," Ellen says. "Where are Mom and Dad?"

"They're getting the car. Said they'll pick us up here."

The parking lot is full, and a long line of vehicles snakes toward the exit. It could be a while before Ellen and Sadie's parents make it over to them. Even after four years of playing soccer for Carlton, Tessa's still sometimes surprised by how many Carlton students and alums turn out for the games. But then again, she always goes to the other teams' games— football, basketball, baseball, tennis, and of course Ellen's track meets. The vast majority of her classmates play at least one sport. It's the main way students can support their small school and show pride in representing their town.

The girls huddle together under Sadie's umbrella as the rain hammers down. Tessa notices that Sadie is wearing red boots that match her umbrella. She's even stylish in the rain.

"Tessa," Sadie says, looking over at her, "I'm really impressed with your game. You're focused and fearless out there, and you've got some amazing footwork. You've come a long way since your freshman year."

Tessa smiles shyly, feeling her face flush. She's been told that she's a skilled player before—she wouldn't have been named captain this year if she weren't—but Sadie plays for Yates University, a small school that has a talented women's soccer team. And Sadie used to be one of the top soccer players at Carlton High. Being complimented by an athlete like Sadie feels meaningful.

Tessa has dreamed of playing college soccer, but their school district is so small that it's difficult for even the most talented student athletes to get on college scouts' radar. Especially since Tessa has only been able to play for her school teams and not any traveling teams. But ever since she joined the team her freshman year, she's been working on her footwork and her shots on her own time. Apparently, it's been paying off.

"I hope you don't mind," Sadie continues, "but I shot some footage of you with my phone. I'd like to show it to my coach back at Yates."

"Really?"

Ellen smiles knowingly at Tessa, and she wonders if Ellen invited Sadie to the game on purpose.

Sadie grins at her. "We could use a player like you on the Yowlers."

"Thank you! That would be amazing." Tessa suddenly feels breathless. "You don't know what this means to me!"

"I can't make any promises, but I know that one of the girls lined up for next year had to drop out of her commitment. Coach Miller is looking to fill the spot if she can."

"They might be able to include a scholarship too," Ellen adds. Sadie doesn't say anything, but Tessa feels herself flush once again. It's no secret that she'd need financial aid to afford school—and she's not ashamed of that—but, for some reason, Sadie knowing that about her feels different.

Tessa clears her throat. "That, ah, that would be great."

Ellen and Sadie's parents pull up along the curb and Sadie steps away. "I'm really gonna push for you, Tessa. I like your game. We'll talk soon!"

"Yeah, of course! Oh, do you have my number—or should I get yours?" Tessa fumbles to pull her phone from her wet sweatshirt pocket. "I'll just . . . oh, the battery died again," she looks up at Sadie sheepishly. "It's an old phone. Doesn't work half the time." She doesn't know why, but she feels like apologizing to Sadie.

She smiles coolly at Tessa and says, "I'll just have Ellen send it to me." She slides into the back seat of the SUV easily—no awkward bumbling with trying to get the umbrella to cooperate as she closes the door. Tessa remembers that during their one year of overlap at Carlton, Sadie was one of the girls who made life seem so easy.

"Tell them I'll be there in a minute," Ellen calls after Sadie.

Tessa turns to Ellen. "Your sister is amazing!"

Ellen snorts. "She can be . . . when she wants to be." Before Tessa can ask her what she means, Ellen grins with excitement. "I can't believe this. Yates!" She grips Tessa's arms and starts jumping up and down. Tessa can't help but join her. "We could be roomies!"

Ellen was already accepted to Yates earlier this fall, with an offer to run for their women's track team. For months, she's been trying to get Tessa to apply too, but until now Tessa didn't think she had a chance to go there.

"What's all the excitement about?" Tessa hears a familiar voice behind her and turns around to see her boyfriend walking over to them. Ellen stiffens next to her, but Tessa pretends not to notice.

"Ben! You made it!" she says. He was supposed to help his parents with work on their farm tonight. She'd been a little disappointed that he wouldn't be there to see what could have been one of her last high school games.

"Can't cut hay in the rain," Ben explains with a smile. "I slipped in just after the second half started." Tessa notices now that he's even still wearing his work clothes, his baseball cap tucked low over his face to keep the rain water away. He must have headed over to the school immediately after finishing his work. Tessa happily rushes over to give him a hug, not minding the fact that they're both soaking wet from the rain.

"Nice shot at the end there," he says, looking down at her.

"You must be my good luck charm!" Tessa says with a grin.

"Nah," Ben says. "You don't need luck— you've got skills."

"OK," Ellen groans. "If you two are going to get all lovey dovey and gross, I'm out of here."

Tessa laughs and steps away from Ben. "Sorry, El. Text me later?"

"Yeah, yeah." Ellen is already walking toward the SUV, clearly annoyed. With a hand on the passenger door, she stops and turns back to Tessa. "I'll let you know if I hear anything from Sadie."

Tessa perks up. "That would be great."

"And, in the meantime, stay focused!"

"I *am* focused," Tessa says, wondering what Ellen could be talking about. But then she sees the way Ellen eyes Ben.

"Not with him around."

BEN and Tessa started dating nearly a year ago, when they were paired together for their chemistry lab. Up until then, Tessa had never paid much attention to him, even though they'd been going to school together since kindergarten. But over the semester she got to know him and realized he was more than just a quiet country boy.

Ben has been naturally athletic since Tessa can remember. He shot up to six feet tall when they were just freshmen. But for some reason, Ben is one of the only kids in their school who never joined a team.

Some people—Ellen included—were shocked that Ben didn't play any sports. "It's practically a betrayal to the school," Ellen said once. "He's got all that natural skill and can't be bothered to do anything with it. It's like he has no school pride at all!" Tessa didn't think it was that big of a deal, though she did wonder why Ben had so little interest in athletics.

In their chemistry class, Tessa and Ben had to work on multiple projects together. They spent afternoons in the library doing research and creating presentations, and eventually they started coming over to each other's houses to study.

In time, Tessa realized that Ben wasn't holding out on sports because of some desire to defy the school and his fellow students. He just isn't interested in sports. He likes books and music—he spends his nights after school teaching himself new songs on guitar. He works on his family farm, where there's always something for him to do. And he's really into science—especially renewable energy. This past summer, he spent nearly every day working with his dad on a project that could bring renewable energy to their farm.

A few weeks into the semester, Tessa found

herself wanting to talk to Ben every day. Ellen didn't get it and teased Tessa constantly for her "weird crush on the quiet kid." Other students stared at them as they walked down the hallway together—and not just because Ben is nearly a head taller than Tessa. She knew some found it weird that a jock like Tessa was hanging around with the one kid at Carlton who actively avoided sports.

But she didn't care. Ben was funny and smart and kind. One day a few weeks before the homecoming dance, she marched up to him in the hall and asked if he'd go with her. They've been together ever since.

Now, three days after the game against the Wildcats, rain pounds against the tin roof as Tessa enters the barn to meet Ben.

She flicks on a light. Empty milking stalls line both sides of a long cement aisle. There's no hay left in the barn except small pieces scattered around the floor, and the scent of manure is gone. Six months ago, Tessa's parents had to sell off their small herd. The price of milk had dropped, and the farm was in debt. It broke all of their hearts when they had to say goodbye to the cows, but at least most went to neighbors. A few even ended up on Ben's farm. All that remains now are the names of the cows written on index cards above the stalls.

The emptiness and silence of the barn still feel strange.

Tessa sighs, standing with her hands on her hips, as she looks around the barn.

The sound of footsteps approaches and the door creaks open. She turns to see Ben stepping through, shaking out his wet hair.

"Hey," she greets as she walks over. The click of her cleats against the bare cement floor echoes throughout the barn. She gives him a quick kiss and smiles up at him. "Thanks for coming over."

He nods and waves a hand back toward the pouring rain outside. "Can't do much else with all this going on anyway."

Tessa leads him toward the hayloft where she practices. She notices Ben eyeing the empty stalls like she was just doing. "I didn't think I'd miss all the chores that went along with the cows, but I do," she says. Her parents are struggling to keep the farm going now. They still have the chickens and fields, but both of her parents had to pick up extra work in town to help make ends meet. Tessa offered to quit soccer and get a part-time job, but her parents refused, knowing how passionate she is about soccer. The chance that she might get an athletic scholarship doesn't hurt either.

"Then you should come over and help me out more," Ben teases. "We could muck out stalls together."

Tessa rolls her eyes at him. "So romantic." He laughs as he follows her up the ladder to the loft.

They walk over to the "net," which isn't really a net, but a large roll of chicken wire and two-by-fours. She and her father put it together a few years ago so she could practice during the winter and on rainy days like this. These days, he seems happy that the barn is still being used for something.

As Tessa pulls her arms behind her head to stretch, Ben asks, "Hey, did you hear from Ellen's sister yet?" She'd told him about what Sadie had said that night, and he took her out for ice cream to celebrate.

"Nothing yet," Tessa says, bringing one arm across her chest and pulling against it with the other. "I'm trying not to think too much about it. We don't know anything yet."

She rolls her shoulders and straightens up. "Besides, I need to focus on this next game over everything else. St. Theresa's has this fantastic goalie—Kellie Jones."

"What's so great about her?" Ben asks as he pulls a soccer ball out of one of the bins Tessa keeps up in the loft.

"Nothing gets past her. She's, like, super tall. She's had *five* shutouts this season alone. She's only a junior and she's already getting offers from schools across the country," Tessa explains. She lowers her gaze and mutters, "Must be nice."

"Hey," Ben says. He wraps an arm around her shoulder. "Your chance is coming.

Besides, I thought you weren't going to think about that."

That brings a smile out of Tessa and she playfully elbows him, stepping away. "I know, I know. It's just—it's hard *not* to think about it. It would be such an amazing opportunity, and my parents wouldn't have to worry about me anymore. Plus, Yates is just an hour away from Woodrow."

Ben plans to go to Woodrow County Technical College next year, though Tessa knows he'd really like to go to Yates too. Yates has an impressive engineering program. But it's an expensive school. Without a scholarship, Tessa doesn't know if she'll even be able to go there. If Yates doesn't work out, her plan is to save money and go to a community college as well. Which is another reason why she's been anxious to hear from Sadie about the Yowlers' team. Until she figures that out, her future is still up in the air.

"C'mon," Ben says, clearly trying to distract her from where her thoughts are going, "let's get started."

"TESSA?" She's been practicing shots with Ben in the goal for half an hour when Ellen's voice interrupts them. "You in there?"

"Hey!" Tessa calls breathlessly. She peers over the edge of the hayloft and waves to Ellen. "Up here. C'mon up!"

Ellen climbs up the ladder quickly and then stops short when she sees Ben is up here too. "Oh. Hey."

He nods once at her. "Ellen."

"You guys still do this?" she asks, gesturing to the net behind them. Ellen hasn't come around to the farm as often since Ben started coming over more.

"Yeah," Tessa says. "He's been helping me with my shot."

"He doesn't even play soccer," Ellen says without looking at him. "How is he going to help you?"

"He's been guarding the net. I've told you that. He makes a good goalie."

Ellen doesn't respond to this but crosses her arms instead. "He was standing wrong anyway," she mutters.

"Well, that's how I stand," Ben says. "If you can kick the ball past me, then you can tell me what to do."

She makes a face back at him. "Please. I could run circles around you. Maybe that wouldn't be the case if you'd actually joined a team at school."

Ben looks past her and toward the door. Tessa can tell he wants to leave now that Ellen is here. Tessa knows he doesn't like her, but he's never said anything bad about her either.

She sighs, wishing the two of them would get along.

"I don't have time," he explains with a tight voice. "I have to help out on our farm."

"Other kids at Carlton live on farms too, but they manage to work *and* play sports," Ellen says, not letting up.

It's been hard for their school to have any success against other teams in their district. She knows it's frustrating for Ellen—who's a fighter on the soccer field *and* runs her heart out for the track team—to see Ben choosing not to contribute. But she also knows Ben is doing more than just field work.

"Ben's doing a huge project," Tessa tries to explain to Ellen. "He and his dad are working on powering their entire farm—"

"With cow poop," Ellen interrupts. "I know, I know. I had to sit through his presentation in physics last week."

"Methane," Ben corrects. "We capture the methane gas and use it to power a turbine that creates the electricity."

"Gross," Ellen says.

"Actually," Ben snaps, "when you capture the methane it makes it so the manure doesn't smell anymore. So really, it's less gross."

Ellen rolls her eyes.

"What Benny and his dad are doing is amazing," Tessa says. "This could have a huge impact on the future of farming." But she knows Ellen doesn't get it and doesn't care.

Everyone is quiet for a moment, and Tessa chews on her lip as she looks from Ellen to Ben. She sighs. "So, did you need something?"

Ellen's eyes light up in excitement again. "I heard from Sadie today—I tried calling you, but you didn't pick up."

"Oh, yeah," Tessa says. "I left my phone in the house."

"What did Sadie say?" Ben asks excitedly.

Ellen eyes him again but then grins anyway. "Not only is Sadie coming back to watch our next game, but she's also bringing her coach with her!"

"Oh my gosh," Tessa squeals. "This is amazing!"

"I know, right?" Ellen says. Then her face shifts slightly. "There's just . . . one thing."

"What is it?"

"Her coach is *technically* coming to see Kellie Jones."

Tessa feels her shoulders drop in disappointment. "Oh."

"But that just means you have to score on her!" Ellen continues. "If you can score on a goalie like Kellie Jones, Yates will definitely take an interest in you."

"Oh really?" Tessa says sarcastically. "That's *all* I have to do? Score on Kellie Jones?"

"Play like you always play," Ben tells her. "You light up the field every game."

"You do," Ellen agrees. "And, hey, Coach Miller may be officially coming to see Kellie, but Sadie said she's going to introduce you too. So this is a good thing!"

"I guess," Tessa admits.

"This is great," Ben says. He grins at her and even Ellen too. "You know what you need to do out there."

Ellen nods enthusiastically. "No pressure, though."

"Sure," Tessa groans. "No pressure at all."

THE next few days, Tessa feels like she's crawling through quicksand. Every class seems so slow. Even practice is painful. Now that she's heard Yates's coach is going to be at the game against St. Theresa's, she just wants it to happen already.

Finally, Thursday evening arrives, and the Carlton Colts and St. Theresa's Royals get to face off.

While Tessa and Ellen are walking to the locker room, Ellen pulls her phone out of her bag. "It's Sadie," she says, reading a text. "They're here."

Tessa suddenly feels nervous—more nervous than she's ever felt in her life. Not only is she trying to help her team make it to the quarterfinals, she now needs to impress Coach Miller.

"Are you okay?" Ellen asks.

"I just need to get out on that field," Tessa says. Once she's on the field, all her focus will be on the game.

"Just breathe," Ellen says. "Don't think about it. This is just a regular game like every other one."

Ben catches up to them before they get inside. "Hey," he says. "Good luck out there tonight. You've got this."

"The coach from Yates is here," Tessa blurts out.

He gives her a small, calming smile. "Like I said—you've got this."

"What if this is my one shot?" she asks. "And what if I screw it all up?"

"You won't," Ellen assures her.

"Show them what you've got," Ben adds.

***

Usually before a game, their coach gives the team a pep talk and then Tessa, as the team captain, steps in and amps up the girls. But this time in the locker room, after Coach Andrea is done, Ellen stands on top of one of the benches before Tessa can say anything.

"Here's the deal," Ellen announces to the team. "We all know that Tessa here is an incredible soccer player—she's scored more goals this season than anyone else has. I think she's one of the best forwards in this state, but no one else has been able to see this. But today, she has a chance. There's a college coach in the stands watching her."

"Technically she's watching Kellie Jones," Tessa adds.

"So," Ellen continues over her, "we need to help her shine, just like she's made this team shine. We all play our best game and get the ball to Tessa. She needs to score."

The other girls cheer and clap Tessa on the back.

"We've got you, T!" one girl says.

"You can do this," another adds.

Tessa looks over at their coach, knowing this is a little unusual. Coach Andrea folds her arms over her clipboard and winks. "Go get 'em, kid."

Some of Tessa's nerves disappear. It feels good to know that everyone on her team will be supporting and looking out for her tonight.

"But more than that," Tessa says then, climbing up on the bench to join Ellen. "We need to play as a team so that we can win and keep going through this season. Who knows, maybe for the first time we'll make it to State!"

The rest of the girls whoop and cheer.

THE two teams head out onto the field. Tessa tries to channel that feeling she had after their last game—that feeling of knowing, just knowing, that her team can win. But she can't find the confidence this time.

As Tessa lines up, she looks down the field and sees Kellie Jones stretching her arms and legs. She's taller than Tessa was expecting. She jokes with one of her teammates as she stretches her calves, as if she doesn't even care that the Yates women's soccer coach is in the stands specifically to watch her play.

The Royals get the kickoff. Tessa and another teammate cover the forwards, but these girls are fast. Smooth. They make beautiful passes back and forth. They bring it down the field, seemingly unstoppable. Finally, Tessa manages to run down a player, intercept a pass, and turn it around.

She sees Ellen sprint to her left just up ahead. She passes Ellen the ball and Ellen passes it to another Colts player.

They move midway into the Royals' half of the field. The ball flies over to Tessa. She can feel Kellie Jones watching her. She fires the ball, but instead of curving it, the ball goes straight and high. Kellie easily stops it.

Tessa clenches her fists in frustration, while Kellie laughs with a nearby teammate. She does a quick little dance, and Tessa hears her say, "Gonna have to do better than that."

"I will, just you wait," Tessa says to herself. She heads back down the field as Kellie boots the ball over her head.

Ellen uses her speed and gets to the ball first. Tessa keeps pace as Ellen charges toward the net, but the Royals' defenders close in, surrounding Tessa. Ellen can't pass her the ball and instead passes it to another teammate. She looks to pass to Tessa as well, but when Tessa still isn't open, her teammate takes the shot herself. The ball sails over the net.

"Gotta get open, Dobbs!" Coach Andrea calls from the sidelines as Tessa jogs past her.

"I'm trying," Tessa pants.

"Try harder. You can't score if you don't have the ball."

Kellie boots the ball down the field again. Tessa and a swarm of Royals race to it, but she's able to kick it out of the way. Ellen pounces on it and takes control of the ball.

Tessa runs after her. "Take a shot!" she shouts when Ellen gets close to the net, but Ellen kicks it wide.

During the next play, the Royals get the ball and take it to the Colts' net.

Tessa chases the ball down, trying to get it away from the Royal who is heading to the net, but their feet get tied up. Tessa tumbles and nearly crashes into a girl.

The Royals' player sends the ball flying into the corner of the net, and they score. Tessa feels a heaviness in her gut, feeling like this goal was her fault.

With only twenty minutes left on the clock, the Royals are ahead 2–1.

The Colts take the kickoff, but the Royals are determined to stop them from moving down the field. When Tessa even touches the ball at least three players swarm her, but Ellen can outrun them all.

She cuts to the middle of the field and races toward the net.

Tessa expects her to take a shot on goal, but, at the last second, Ellen passes the ball back to her. A Royals player intercepts it and kicks the ball out-of-bounds.

Tessa is awarded the corner kick.

She stands near the flag and looks at the net. She can see the curve and angle she needs in her head, but there's a crowd of players in front of the net. Kellie Jones, tall and focused, watches and waits.

Tessa backs up and takes the kick. The ball goes high and curves toward the net. She runs toward the players crowded in front of the net and sees Ellen leap up and head the ball. It goes right into the net.

"Yes!" Tessa cheers, throwing her hands above her head.

The game is tied up, 2–2. Tessa hugs Ellen and, for the first time in the entire game, she feels her confidence coming back.

THERE are just five minutes left in the game when the Royals take a shot on the Colts' goalie. The ball hits the bar and bounces back, landing right in front of one of Tessa's teammates. She blasts the ball up the field. Tessa and a Royals defender race to it and battle for the ball. Eventually, Tessa gets control of it.

She sprints to the net, where Kellie is waiting. Just as Tessa is about to take a shot, she gets pushed from behind. Hard. She stumbles and falls into the goal box, right at Kellie's feet.

The referee blows her whistle and calls for a penalty kick.

Reaching down, Kellie helps Tessa up.

"Come on," Kellie says with a competitive smile. "Let's see what you've got."

Tessa walks to where the referee has placed the ball, trying not to think about Kellie Jones or Coach Miller or even winning this game. She imagines herself back up in the hayloft. She's practiced this shot a thousand times. She tells herself she knows what to do. Everything around her goes quiet.

The referee blows her whistle. Tessa takes three steps and kicks the side of the ball. It spins forward through the air. Kellie advances, but then the ball curves to the left and when she lunges for it, it is just out of reach.

The ball goes in.

Tessa feels a rush of energy move through her body. Everything around her grows loud again. She can her the crowd. She can hear her teammates. They surround her in a hug.

"It isn't over," she warns them. "We still have three minutes left."

The Royals line up and boot the ball down the field. Everyone runs for it. Ellen charges ahead of the group and wins the race to the ball. She sprints down the sideline with the ball, and Tessa runs next to her, guarding her. They keep control of the ball until the end-of-game buzzer goes off.

Tessa's teammates cheer all around her. Ellen crushes her in a hug, but Tessa looks over to Kellie Jones instead. She looks disappointed, but when she notices Tessa watching her, she gives her a nod.

The other girls on the field don't seem to notice, but Tessa returns Kellie's nod of respect.

AS they head back to the locker room to
celebrate, Tessa sees Coach Miller talking to the
Royals coach and Kellie Jones. Even though her
team won the game, Tessa can't help but wonder
what they're talking about, what Coach Miller
thought of Kellie's playing. Is she impressed?
How does she think Tessa played in comparison?

Sadie jogs over to them, interrupting her
thoughts. "Another great game, Tessa Dobbs!"

Tessa can't quite bring herself to give
them a full smile. Her eyes are still locked on
where Coach Miller is talking to Kellie. Sadie
looks over her shoulder and sees where Tessa
is looking.

"Don't worry about it," she assures. "This
was a scheduled visit. Plus, Jones is still a

junior. She wouldn't be the one taking that spot next year anyway."

That does make Tessa feel slightly better. But now she's left wondering how many other players Coach Miller has been meeting with to fill this spot.

"We'll talk again soon," she hears Coach Miller say as she and the Royals coach shake hands. After Kellie and her coach walk away, Sadie leads Tessa over to Coach Miller.

Ellen hangs back, pretending like she's not trying to listen to their every word.

"Coach," Sadie says with a grin, "this is the fabulous Tessa Dobbs."

Tessa reaches for Coach Miller's hand and gives what she hopes is an impressive handshake.

Coach Miller isn't as friendly as Tessa was expecting her to be. Rather than giving Tessa a smile, she's reserved. Her eyes give away nothing as she looks Tessa up and down. Tessa clears her throat nervously, wanting to look away but forcing herself not to.

"You're smaller than I thought," Coach Miller eventually says.

"Yes, ma'am," Tessa responds, not knowing what else to say. Then she adds, "But I'm solid. Strong."

The coach hums thoughtfully at that. "Sadie tells me you haven't committed to a school for next year yet."

"Not yet."

"What traveling team do you play on?" she asks.

"I don't," Tessa responds, trying not to stutter. "I mean, I haven't . . ."

She doesn't get to explain. Coach Miller is already on the next question. "Any training camps?"

Tessa shakes her head.

"So," Coach Miller says, "you've just played high school soccer?"

"And in the hayloft," Tessa says, immediately realizing how strange that sounds. She sees Sadie look at her awkwardly as if she's suddenly embarrassed by Tessa.

Tessa tries to explain quickly, "Every day I work on my footwork and practice my shot. My dad set up a place for me to practice up in our barn. But anyway, I try to take a hundred shots a day." She babbles, trying to explain how hard she's worked over the past four years, how the hard work has improved her game.

Coach Miller just moves on. "Well, I like that you haven't been influenced by too many coaches," she says. "I'd have less bad coaching to undo."

"She's an incredible player." Tessa hears Coach Andrea's voice from behind her.

"I'm not the most experienced soccer coach in the world," Coach Andrea admits with a laugh as she shakes Coach Miller's hand. "But I have to tell you, Tessa Dobbs is a gifted player. She came up with that shot of hers all on her own."

Coach Miller nods at this. She turns to Tessa. "How about you come make a visit to Yates? I'd like to talk some more with you, and—" she turns to Sadie, "I'm sure Sadie here would love to show you around our campus."

Tessa can feel her eyes grow wide, tempted to lunge forward and hug both Coach Miller and Sadie. But Coach Miller doesn't look like someone who enjoys hugs, so she restrains herself and says, "I'd love to visit Yates, thank you. You've created a really dynamic team."

"Yes, I have," Coach Miller says with a proud smile. "Thanks to talent like Sadie. She's one of our top players. We'll have to have you watch a practice too."

"That would be great," Tessa breathes, unable to believe all of this is actually happening.

Coach Miller pulls out a business card from her pocket. "Here's my card. Send me an email and we'll get your visit scheduled. Stay in touch with Sadie too."

Sadie nods enthusiastically and grins again at Tessa.

"OK," Tessa says, taking the card and staring at it in her hand. It looks so official.

"Nice game tonight," Coach Miller says to her. As she turns, she nods to Coach Andrea. "Coach. Great team you've got here."

Tessa watches, still in shock, as Coach Miller walks into the parking lot. Coach Andrea laughs, pats Tessa on the back, and walks off too. Ellen races up to where Sadie and Tessa are still standing. "Oh. My. Gosh," she squeals, wrapping her arms around both of them. "That was awesome. She *totally* wants you to come play for her team, I just know it!"

Tessa laughs shakily. "We don't know that."

"Well, she asked you to come visit the school, right?" Ellen looks over to her sister. "That's got to be a good sign?"

Sadie nods. "Definitely." She meets Tessa's eyes with a serious look. "You got your foot in the door, now you just need to wow her with this visit. And you need to wow my sorority too."

Sorority? Tessa thinks. Before she can ask Sadie any questions, Ben calls out to her. Tessa runs over to him and leaps into his arms. "I got invited to visit Yates!"

"Of course you did," Ben says. "You were amazing out there."

"Who is that?" Tessa hears Sadie ask Ellen.

"Tessa's boyfriend," Ellen explains.

Tessa pulls away from Ben, suddenly embarrassed. As she introduces them, she swears she sees Sadie wrinkle her nose.

OVER the next two weeks, the Colts play three more games. They lose one but win two, meaning they'll qualify for the quarterfinals in two weeks. But first, Tessa has to shift her focus to another team.

On Saturday, Ben picks up Tessa in his truck, and they bounce down a gravel road with the radio turned up and the windows down. It's a warm fall morning. They turn onto a highway and head to town. They have to pick up Ellen too since she insisted on coming along. Tessa's parents can't make the trip because they both have to work, so she's happy to have the company.

They pull up in front of Ellen's house, where she's sitting on the front steps, wearing a pink dress with a white denim jacket and sandals. Tessa looks down at her clothes. Sadie had told her she should dress nicely, so she put on her best pair of jeans and a button up shirt. At the time, she'd thought that would be enough, but seeing Ellen in a dress makes her wonder if she made a mistake.

She thinks about asking Ben if they can stop back at her place so she can put on something fancier, but the clock on his dashboard shows they're already running ten minutes late.

"Let's go!" Ben shouts lightheartedly as Ellen takes her time walking up to the truck. He honks the horn. "We're late as it is!"

Ellen ignores that and says, "Let's take my car."

"We need to take Ben's," Tessa explains.

"Why?"

"I'm bringing something in the back of my truck to show a professor at Yates," he explains. "I've been emailing him the last few months. I arranged to meet with him while you girls are with Sadie."

Ellen takes a step away from the truck. "Please tell me it isn't a bin of cow poop."

"No, it's not manure."

"Well, something sure smells like it," she says flatly.

Ben sighs. "I swear, I don't have a load of it in the back."

"Come on," Tessa says. "We don't have time for this. Just hop in."

"Just move whatever you have into my car," Ellen tries.

"It's too heavy," Ben says. "It's an engine I want to power with a fuel cell."

Ellen peers into the passenger window of his truck, then looks down at her dress and lets out a long groan.

"Fine. Move over," she tells Tessa, hopping into the truck. Tessa scoots over next to Ben. "It smells like a farm in here," Ellen says, plugging her nose.

Tessa rolls her eyes. Sometimes her friend can be so difficult.

Ben pulls the truck away from the curb. "You'll get used to it."

Three hours later, Yates's bell tower rises in the distance. Tessa and Ellen lean forward in the truck as they approach the school.

"I cannot wait to go here," Ellen sighs.

There are dozens of buildings surrounded by large oak trees and green lawns. Down the hill from the school is a huge football stadium. Ellen explains that the smaller stadium right next to it is just for soccer.

"They sure love their sports here," Ben says.

"Yes, they do," Ellen replies. "But it's also one of the top academic schools in the Midwest."

"Yeah, they have a great engineering program," he adds.

Ellen looks over at him in surprise.

"I'm talking to a professor here, obviously I've researched the place," Ben points out. "I'd go here if I could afford it."

Ellen just shakes her head. Tessa knows what she is thinking—if Ben had participated in sports then maybe he'd have an athletic scholarship to go here too.

They drive past students walking, biking, and skateboarding around campus.

"Turn here," Ellen says, pointing to a street. "Sadie wants us to meet her at her sorority house first. Then she'll bring us over to the soccer stadium."

As they turn the corner, Ben's truck begins to make a strange screeching noise. Ellen covers her face with her hands.

"Well, at least we made it," Ben says as he pulls into a parking spot on the street and pops the hood of his truck.

Ellen and Tessa get out of the truck and see Sadie, dressed in red soccer warmups, standing on the front porch of her sorority house. It's a big white house with two Greek letters painted in gold on the front.

"Omega Phi," Ellen explains to Tessa. "Whatever you do, don't mess that up. They get offended if you mess up the name of their house."

"Yeah, Ellen," Tessa begins, "I've been meaning to ask you, what are we doing at Sadie's sorority house? I thought I was just here to watch the team and see the school."

Before Ellen can answer, they hear Sadie's voice from the front of the house. "Ellen? What in the world?"

Sadie slowly makes her way down the steps with a tight smile on her face. She hugs the girls but keeps her eyes on Ben's truck the whole time.

"I'm so glad you're here," she says and then wrinkles her nose. "But you both smell a bit like a farm."

"Tessa's boyfriend insisted on driving," Ellen says. "I offered to drive, but they wouldn't listen."

"Ben has this project he's working on in the back of the truck," Tessa tries to explain.

"He makes electricity out of cow poop," Ellen adds.

"Methane!" Ben yells from under the hood of his truck.

Sadie looks over at Ben. "Is he coming with us?"

"He's meeting with a professor," Tessa says, following Sadie's stare.

"Oh." Sadie gives a true smile, looking

relieved. "Good." She turns and calls to Ben, "Do you want me to call you a tow truck or something?"

He pops his head out from under the hood. "Nah, I'm good." Then he looks over at Tessa. "I'll meet up with you later, OK?"

"You have grease on your face," Ellen says.

"I'll text you when we're done," Tessa tells Ben, ignoring her.

Sadie looks at her phone. "We'd better go," she says to Ellen and Tessa. "I told Coach Miller I'd have you there before our practice starts."

Tessa grabs her soccer bag out of the back of Ben's truck and gives him a quick kiss goodbye.

"Good luck," he says.

"You too." She hopes this professor can help him out. Ben has big plans to run the trucks and tractors on his family's farm on fuel cells powered by the methane.

Sadie leads them to her jeep. Ellen crawls in the back and gives Tessa the front seat.

As Sadie pulls out of her parking space,

she tells Tessa and Ellen she has a surprise for them after practice.

"What is it?" Ellen asks.

"You'll see," Sadie says with a knowing grin.

SADIE points out the different sorority and fraternity houses as they drive down the street.

"Sixty percent of Yates students are part of the Greek system," Sadie points out. "Greek life is great because once you leave college, you always have a network of sisters and brothers. And the women of Omega Phi are known as leaders. Did you know that some of the top female CEOs are Omega Phi sisters?"

"No, I didn't," Tessa says. She's never thought about joining a sorority. Is this why Ellen wanted them to stop by the sorority house?

Ellen leans forward between the seats. "I sure hope I get into Omega Phi next year."

Sadie looks at Ellen in the rearview mirror and gives a weird smile. "I sure hope you do too."

Tessa looks at Sadie and back at Ellen, wondering why Ellen *wouldn't* be able to join her own sister's sorority.

As they drive across campus, Sadie points out the other buildings—the Student Union, various academic buildings, some dorms. The soccer stadium is at the far end of campus.

"Last year, we got a brand new workout facility," Sadie explains, pointing to a small building in between both stadiums. "It's just for the athletes on school teams. Open to us twenty-four hours a day."

"That's awesome," Ellen says. She leans forward again and says to Tessa, "We can work out there together next year!"

"And," Sadie continues with a proud smirk, "there's a smoothie bar."

Ellen gasps, this time grabbing at Tessa's arm. "We can get smoothies *every day!*"

Tessa nods, trying to keep up with Ellen's excitement. *A smoothie bar and private weight room* are *cool*, she thinks. *But, right now, all I want is to see some soccer.*

When they enter the stadium, Sadie leads

them down to the field. The grass and white lines seem brighter and cleaner than any field Tessa has ever played on. On the far end is a large scoreboard with a jumbo screen. Rather than the bleachers Tessa is used to seeing, the crowd seating is made up of rows of red and white chairs.

Sadie takes them to the locker room where her teammates have started to gather for practice. The girls smile and wave at Sadie as she passes. She leads Tessa and Ellen to Coach Miller's office.

"I'll be honest with you," Sadie says in a low voice, "Coach has already been meeting with other girls. But some of our top prospects have chosen other schools. So the spot is still available, but you have to prove that you're the best choice."

"Thanks again for everything," Tessa says.

"Just don't embarrass me," Sadie says, her voice suddenly turning cold. "I've put my neck out for you."

"She won't," Ellen snaps at her sister. "What is wrong with you?"

"I'm just trying to stress the importance of following through."

Tessa just nods at this, beginning to feel overwhelmed.

"Well," Sadie says, giving her a stiff hug, "good luck."

Tessa and Ellen watch Sadie head back to the locker room.

"I'll be in the stands when you're done," Ellen says.

"Thanks for coming with me today," Tessa says.

"Of course," Ellen says. Then she glances over her shoulder before leaning in and whispering, "Just . . . stay in my sister's good graces. She's a little intense sometimes, but she has a good heart."

Tessa nods again, though she doesn't know what Ellen means. She thought Sadie liked her.

She tries to shake these thoughts off as she knocks on Coach Miller's door.

When Tessa walks into the office, she sees that there are two assistant coaches here too. They all watch her sit down.

Coach Miller introduces Tessa to the other coaches before opening a folder on her desk. Tessa can't see much of it but she can tell it's all her information.

"So, we've looked over your transcript," Coach Miller says. "Solid. That's important here. Yates puts academics first."

Tessa nods for a moment, then realizes they're waiting for her to say something in response. She flushes. "Ah, yeah, school was always really important to my parents. And my high school is small, but that also helped keep a balance between homework and practices."

"Stats are good," one of the assistant coaches comments to the others. "Her team plays for a small conference, but they're doing well this year."

"We actually just qualified for the state quarterfinals," she explains. "It's our team's first time going."

Coach Miller hums in approval but keeps her eyes on the pages in front of her as she looks through them. "All right, Tessa, we're going to have you watch the team practice this afternoon. Then I'd like you to run a few drills with my assistant coaches to see where your skills are."

"Great," Tessa says, pointing to her bag. "I brought my cleats."

THE passing drills the Yowlers' players run are impressive. So are the techniques the forwards use when shooting on the net.

After watching practice for a while, Tessa works with one of the assistant coaches through basic soccer skills and plays. He has her shoot into the net over and over again, making notes on his clipboard each time. He doesn't say much, so Tessa can't tell how she's doing.

Finally, Coach Miller comes over to them. "How are things going?" she asks the assistant coach without even glancing at Tessa.

"Good," the assistant coach says, handing her the notes on his clipboard. "Ms. Dobbs has a great shot."

"Yes, she does," Coach Miller agrees. "But she needs to get a bit more power behind it."

Tessa doesn't like the way they're speaking about her as if she isn't there. *Is this the way she always talks about her players?* Tessa can't help but wonder. "I can work on that," she says.

The coach says something quietly to her assistant, and Tessa can tell by the look on her face that the tryout is over. "Thanks for coming out today, Tessa," Coach Miller says, finally turning to her. "We'll be in touch."

"Ah—thank you," Tessa responds, accepting Coach Miller's handshake when she reaches over. She doesn't really know what she's supposed to do now.

Coach Miller watches her with amusement. "Listen, you've made a good impression on me, and not many people do."

It's the first time the coach has said something to her that seems genuine. Tessa gives a true smile this time and adds another "thanks."

Coach Miller looks down at the clipboard in her hands and waves it. "We'll be in touch," she says again. "In the meantime, take good care of yourself and keep working."

"I will! Definitely!" Tessa bites on her lip, hoping she didn't sound too eager just now. The coach is already walking back to her players on the other side of the field, so she doesn't seem to notice.

Tessa looks up and sees Ellen clapping for her in the stands.

"How do you think it went?" Ellen asks as Tessa sits down next to her.

"Well, she said she was impressed by me," Tessa says. "So that has me a little stunned." She gives a nervous laugh.

"That's great!" Ellen says. "You looked really good out there."

"Now all I can do is wait," Tessa adds.

She tries to imagine herself down on that field, but she can't quite see it. Not yet.

SADIE finds them again after practice. Tessa waits for Sadie to ask how everything went, maybe even mention if she heard anything from the other coaches, but she just smiles at them and says, "Now I can tell you all about our special treat for tonight!"

"What is it?" Ellen asks.

"You two are going to join us at the house for a special dinner. I planned it just for you! I want the girls to get to know you so that when you rush next year, you're already familiar faces."

"Rush?" Tessa asks.

"Before you can officially join a sorority, you have to rush. You attend social events and visit the houses. It gives the sororities a chance to get to know you. I'm giving you two a head start."

Sadie leads them through the stadium and back to where her jeep is parked. Tessa trails slightly behind her and Ellen, trying to keep up with what Sadie is talking about. Ellen never mentioned to her that Sadie expected her to join her sorority too. Tessa doesn't even know if she'd want to.

"Omega Phi is the hardest sorority to get into on campus because it's the best," Sadie continues in a bubbly voice. "Obviously."

Tessa can't help but roll her eyes at that.

"So, you two have to make a great impression. Plus, I'm in line to be president of our house next year, and I want to leave a legacy of drawing smart, impressive women into our house. I know that you two will do great things in your future."

As Tessa takes this all in, Ellen squeals and grabs her sister's arms. Tessa, on the other hand, hasn't even applied to Yates yet, let alone decided what groups she might want to join at the school.

Her phone buzzes in her pocket and she sees that Ben is calling. "Hang on," she tells the others. "It's Ben."

"Ugh, doesn't he know how to give a little space?" Sadie grumbles.

Tessa frowns and says, "He's probably just wondering how the practice went."

"Whatever," Sadie says. "Tell him you'll call him later. We have more to discuss in the car!"

"I . . . OK." Tessa declines the call and sends Ben a quick text, saying she'll talk to him soon.

As she jogs to catch up with Sadie and Ellen, she hears Sadie say, "I'm just saying, she can totally do better than a boy like that."

"But you don't even know him," Ellen interrupts.

"I saw him," Sadie says. Tessa has caught up to them, but Sadie keeps talking. "And first impressions are important. He looked like he just fell off the back of his truck."

"He's actually a smart guy," Ellen says, surprising Tessa. "You just need to get to know him."

Sadie waves a hand, brushing her off. "I don't want to get to know him." She takes Tessa's hands in hers. "If you want to go to Yates, then you need to take my advice. I have a lot of pull with Coach Miller. She trusts me, so you need to trust me too."

Sadie turns to lead the way out of the stadium. "Now let's get going. I want to give you both makeovers before dinner tonight!"

Tessa and Ellen quietly follow Sadie to her car.

***

In Sadie's room at the Omega Phi house, Sadie blasts music that Tessa doesn't even like as she plugs in her blow dryer, straightener, and curling iron. Tessa's curly hair gets blown and straightened. Sadie digs out a huge tub of makeup and insists on applying it to Tessa and Ellen.

By the time Tessa looks at herself in Sadie's mirror, she doesn't even recognize herself. She's never worn her hair like this before, and the makeup is much heavier than what she'd normally go with. She usually doesn't mind getting dressed up for special occasions, but this doesn't feel the same—she's never been done up so much that she doesn't even feel like herself.

"What do you think?" Sadie asks.

"I—I don't know," Tessa admits. "It feels like a little . . . much?"

Sadie's and Ellen's faces drop, and she rushes to correct herself. "I mean, it's just different from what I usually do."

"You look great," Sadie insists.

Tessa touches her hair. It's stiff and heavy with product.

"You look like a model," Ellen says, beaming at her.

This makes Tessa blush. She looks in the mirror again. Her hair does look nice and shiny when it's this straight. But it doesn't feel like her hair.

She can tell that's not what Sadie and Ellen want to hear though. "Your hair looks good," she says to them both instead.

Sadie beams at this and turns to look at

herself in the mirror, puffing up her hair even more. "Now, let's talk clothes," she says. She looks at Tessa's duffel bag sitting by the door. "I'm guessing you didn't pack a dress and heels in there too?"

"Ah, no," Tessa says, flicking a glance over to Ellen. "I didn't know I was supposed to."

"That's fine, you can borrow something from me. You're shorter than I am, but I'm sure we can make something work." Sadie walks over to her closet and then eyes Ellen. "We might need to find something for you too."

"What's wrong with this?" Ellen asks, pulling at the skirt of her dress.

"You're kidding, right?" Sadie says. Her voice is teasing, but Tessa can see the hurt it causes Ellen. She's pretty sure Ellen has worn that dress to several birthday parties and team dinners, so clearly it's one of her favorite outfits.

"Like I said," Sadie continues, oblivious to the look on Ellen's face, "you need to make a good first impression on these girls. I just want to help you make friends next year."

"I don't need help making friends," Ellen snaps at her sister. "I have lots of friends."

"She was just homecoming queen," Tessa adds. "Practically everyone at school voted for her."

"Homecoming queen *of Carlton*," Sadie laughs. As she continues to browse through her closet, Ellen turns to Tessa and makes a face.

"I'm thirsty," she says suddenly. "Tessa, let's run downstairs and grab some waters."

"Get me one too!" Sadie calls from the closet.

As Tessa follows Ellen down the stairs, she turns and links arms with Tessa. "I can't stand her sometimes," Ellen hisses. "She's so competitive and mean."

Tessa doesn't say anything. But seeing Sadie behaving like this makes it easier for her to understand Ellen's treatment of Ben. *She's learned all of this from Sadie,* Tessa realizes. It makes her happy that Ellen isn't as bad as her sister.

Although I don't know if I would be friends

with Ellen if she acted like that.

That thought makes her pause while Ellen grabs some water bottles from the fridge. If she wouldn't want to be friends with Ellen if she acted like Sadie, does she really want to be friends with Sadie?

For the first time, Tessa questions if she really does want to go to Yates after all.

***

When they get back to Sadie's room, Tessa checks her phone and sees that Ben has texted her back.

She texts him again and tells him they're getting ready for dinner. She's not sure how she's going to explain that he's not invited because Sadie doesn't want him around.

She glances at herself in the mirror again and tries to convince herself that she could get used to this new look. Her hair doesn't quite shock her anymore—in fact, she could argue that her long, straight hair makes her face look less round. Not that she was ever worried about it looking "too round" before.

Sadie loans them each a dress and heels. The dress Tessa wears is tight and short, so short that she wonders how someone as tall as Sadie could possibly pull off wearing it. The heels are a little loose, and they're much taller than any Tessa has ever worn before.

After Sadie gets changed, she insists the three of them take photos together in front of the house. When they step outside, Tessa sees Ben sitting on the front steps reading a book. He doesn't even look up as they walk past him.

"Let's go!" Sadie cheers, pulling out her cellphone. "Dinner is in half an hour."

Then she turns to Ben and puts on a fake smile. "Sorry, girls only."

Ellen gives Ben an apologetic look and follows Sadie over to a large oak tree by the side of the house.

"Hey," Tessa says to Ben.

He does a double take when he looks up at her. "Whoa," he says. "What happened to all your curls?"

"We, um, we straightened them," Tessa says shyly, lightly touching the tips of her hair and suddenly feeling self-conscious. "What do you think?"

He stares at her for a moment. "You look different."

"Is that good or bad?" Tessa asks.

"Uh, well . . ." Ben stutters. "I mean, I like how you look normally, but you look really nice right now too."

Tessa looks at him and sees what Sadie sees: A tall, thin boy wearing a dirty trucker hat and a pair of old jeans—a boy who looks like he just stepped off a tractor. Then she looks past him to where Sadie is tiptoeing through the grass, trying not to get her heels stuck.

"I have to go to this dinner at the house," she tells him. "Sadie could make or break my chances of getting on the soccer team. She has a lot of pull with the coach."

Ben looks over at Sadie too. Tessa can't help but wonder what he thinks about her, what he might think about Tessa if she became someone like that.

"I know this is kind of silly," she admits, tugging her dress down where it's ridden up.

"But I'm trying to do whatever she wants right now so she'll put in a good word for me."

He nods understandingly. "Well, get over there then."

Tessa feels her shoulders sag with relief. She grins at him. "Honestly, I'd rather change back into my old clothes and get pizza with you instead."

"Nah," he says. "I'll be fine. Besides, that professor I was talking to invited me to have dinner with him and some of his grad students. I'd wanted to check with you first, but I guess I can make it after all."

"That's great," Tessa says, feeling relieved. But suddenly she imagines them doing this next year—for the next four years, in fact. Her not being "allowed" to invite him to things because of Sadie, and him having to make other plans to work around her schedule all the time. Not exactly ideal.

As he gets up to head to his truck, she realizes she didn't even ask him about his meeting yet. She chases after him down the sidewalk and asks him how it went.

"He seemed really interested in what I'm doing," Ben says. "Said he thinks I'd have potential for their engineering department. He's gonna see if there are any scholarships I could apply for."

"You'd go to Yates?"

"Yeah." He laughs at the look of surprise on her face, and Tessa instantly feels terrible.

She shakes her head, then steps forward and hugs him. "That's amazing!" she says. "I'm proud of you."

He tries to brush it off, but she sees him smile to himself. "Thanks." He waves a hand toward the house. "Now go—do what you need to do."

Tessa watches him drive away before walking back to join Sadie and Ellen in the yard where they're taking selfies. They look like they're having a good time, but Tessa could swear Sadie flashes her an annoyed look. Ellen calls her over for a photo and Sadie's face is instantly back to normal.

AFTER enough photos that Tessa's face feels sore, the girls head back into the house.

"So, Tessa," Sadie says, linking arms with her, "how long have you been dating that boy?"

Ellen sends Tessa a look of caution—*tread carefully*. Not that she needs the hint. Sadie's voice may sound casual, but Tessa can hear the underlying tension.

"Ben," she explains. "And about a year now."

Sadie nods thoughtfully. "Have you two talked about what you're going to do next fall?"

"Not exactly," Tessa says. "Although that's mostly because I still don't know what I'm doing next year."

"So it's not serious."

"Sadie," Ellen snaps. "Enough about Ben.

Leave it alone."

"I was just—"

"And actually," Tessa carries on over Sadie, pulling her arm away, "he might apply here. He could be eligible for a scholarship."

"You're kidding," Sadie says. "Well, all the better to break up with him ASAP. He'll only hold you back here." She suddenly smiles as a sorority sister comes up the sidewalk.

Tessa can't tell if Sadie is kidding or serious. She watches her hug the other young woman, acting warm and friendly again.

Ellen shoots Tessa a worried look. Tessa frowns. If Ellen is concerned about her sister's behavior, that can't be a good sign.

***

Ellen and Tessa stand in the middle of the living room as they are introduced to the rest of Sadie's sorority sisters. They both smile and make small talk for close to an hour.

Finally, they find themselves alone for a moment while they refill their cups with lemonade from a pitcher in the kitchen.

"My cheeks hurt," Tessa whispers.

"So do mine," Ellen says. She takes a sip of her lemonade. "I feel like I'm trying too hard. Am I trying to hard? I don't want to seem over eager."

Tessa picks at the lip of her cup. "So you really want to be a part of this next year?"

"Yeah," Ellen says. "It really is the best sorority on campus."

"Wouldn't, like, every sorority say that?"

Ellen stares at her for a moment before they burst into laughter. "OK," Ellen admits. "Maybe that's true. But it's still a really good sorority. I wouldn't want to be in any other one."

Before Tessa can mention how uncertain she's been feeling, Sadie's loud laughter carries into the kitchen as she walks over to them. The moment she's out of earshot of the girls in the living room, she hisses to Tessa and Ellen, "What are you two doing in here, standing by yourselves? The girls will think you're being weird if you're in here much longer."

"We were just taking a break," Ellen says.

Sadie pulls on their arms. "Come sit with me on the couch."

"We will," Ellen says. "In a minute. We were just . . . admiring the kitchen. Love the granite countertops."

Two girls walk past as Ellen says this, and that seems to satisfy Sadie for the moment. She puts on a wide, fake smile again. "Aren't they great?" she asks, a little too loudly. She follows the other girls into the next room.

"Before we go back," Ellen says, "I have to tell you—while you were talking to Ben earlier, Sadie told me Coach Miller emailed her about you. It sounds like she's seriously considering you!"

"Wow," Tessa says, feeling her head start to spin at the thought. "And now Ben might be able to go here too."

"Yeah," Ellen says, but that worried look comes across her face again.

"What is it?"

"I think Sadie might want you to break up with Ben if you want to pledge Omega Phi," Ellen says quietly.

It's not exactly a surprise to Tessa, but hearing it out loud still stings. "What if I don't?" she asks. "I don't even know if I want to pledge a sorority at all."

"Well, I'm sure she won't be happy," Ellen says. "And if you make the team, she'll feel like you owe her. She'll make your life miserable if you don't do what she wants. She'd probably come up with some way to get you kicked off the team."

"Seriously?" Tessa asks. "How could she be that petty? Especially if she wants the team to do well and thinks I'm an asset."

"Hey, you didn't live with her all your life," Ellen says. "I'm just telling you from my experience. Sadie cares about being in control more than anything else."

Tessa steps closer to the living room doorway and watches Sadie across the room for a moment. Sadie is in the middle of a conversation with several other girls. But when she looks over at them and gives another too-big smile, Tessa knows what Ellen is telling her is true.

DINNER isn't quite as fancy as Tessa was expecting, especially considering how dressed up all the girls are. But she realizes quickly that sororities in the movies aren't very realistic frames of reference. Several of the younger girls cooked the dinner, and everyone helps themselves before sitting down at the long table in the dining room.

Ellen and Tessa both sit between two girls from the sorority. The girls sitting next to Tessa are nice enough. They ask her about where she's from and what she might want to study in college next year, but as the meal goes on, Tessa realizes she has nothing in common with either of them. She tries to listen to a conversation between some of the other girls sitting across from her, but she's not interested in anything they talk about either.

She glances down the table and sees Ellen laughing and joking with the girl next to her. Sadie, who sits two seats away from Tessa, watches her sister approvingly.

When the girl sitting between them excuses herself to get a glass of water, Sadie slides over to the seat next to Tessa. "So, what do you think?" she asks.

Tessa chews slowly to give herself more time to think. "It seems like a great school," she says finally. "And the soccer program—it's great. Coach Miller seems really great too." She's suddenly aware that she's saying "great" too many times.

"She is," Sadie agrees. She continues to look at Tessa, as if waiting for her to say more. Some of the other girls are listening in now too.

"And your sorority," Tessa continues. "Everyone is so nice." The girls grin at her. "And, um, this food is amazing."

Sadie is clearly pleased. "So you feel like you can see yourself here? Like you belong here?"

Tessa thinks she can see herself on the soccer field and sitting in a classroom at Yates. But, if she's being honest, she can't see herself being a part of this sorority. She definitely can't see herself walking past Ben on campus and having to ignore him.

"Yeah," she lies, and then takes a bite of food to avoid having to say anything else.

"Good," Sadie says. "I can see you here too—on the field, in this house, maybe with a new boyfriend."

Tessa chokes at that. She tries to swallow and cough at the same time, hastily reaching for her glass of lemonade. She chugs it down before she even realizes that everyone is watching her.

Sadie raises an eyebrow at her but says nothing. Tessa smiles sheepishly, even though what she really wants to do is puke.

***

Finally, dinner is over and Ellen and Tessa are free to go, after Ellen promises she'll return their borrowed outfits later.

"I don't think I can do this," Tessa says as they head to Ben's truck. He's sitting in the front seat, listening to music. "I'm not going to break up with Ben just to please your sister."

"You don't have to do it right away."

Tessa doesn't say anything in response as Ben waves to them.

"You don't have to decide anything right now," Ellen continues. "Just think about everything for a while. Make a list of pros and cons or something. And don't throw this away just because of a high school boy."

They climb into the truck, and Ben asks how dinner was. Ellen gives him a small smile, but Tessa can't even answer.

The ride home is quiet. Ellen falls asleep with her head against the window. Ben reaches down to hold Tessa's hand, but she pulls it away. She can't breathe sitting in the middle of Ben and Ellen.

"Can you roll down your window?" she asks him.

"Sure." As he does, he glances over at her.

Tessa swallows heavily. "I don't feel good."

"Want me to pull over?"

"Yeah," she says. "I need to get out of this truck."

He pulls over on a dirt road. Ellen wakes up. "Are we home?" she asks.

"I need to get out," Tessa says, hearing the panic in her own voice. Her fingers grip the dashboard in front of her. "I need to get out now."

Ellen opens the door and Tessa scrambles out. She starts walking down the road. Ellen follows her.

"You need to calm down," Ellen says.

"I can't break up with Ben just so I can play for the Yates soccer team," Tessa bursts out. "I can't imagine having to see him on campus and know that I can't be with him anymore. He's not just my boyfriend, he's my best friend." As the words come out, she sees the hurt on Ellen's face.

"I thought I was your best friend."

"A best friend wouldn't tell me to break up with my boyfriend so I can play soccer and join some sorority."

"It isn't just about soccer or the sorority," Ellen says. "This is about your future. Yates is a great school, and playing for the Yowlers could even get you a scholarship. A *scholarship*! How else are you going to get an opportunity like this?"

Tessa stays quiet. She doesn't know.

Ellen sighs. "Look, I know you're happy with Ben. I know I give him a hard time, but he's actually a pretty nice guy." Tessa looks over at her in surprise. That has to be the nicest thing Ellen has ever said about Ben.

She waves her hand, clearly not wanting to draw too much attention to it. "But," she continues, "I don't think you should throw away such an incredible chance just for him. Going to Yates could open doors for the rest of your life. Don't you get it?"

"I do," Tessa hears Ben say. Both girls turn to see him standing a few feet away.

"BEN," Tessa says. But he turns on his heel and walks back to his truck. She stumbles after him, trying to catch up. She pauses for a moment to pull the heels off her feet.

"Ben," she repeats, catching up to him. "Let me explain. Please."

Ben turns around but doesn't look at her. He looks past her to the fields. "There's nothing to explain," he says. "You do what you need to do."

"I don't know what I want to do," she says. "I just know that I want to play soccer and I want to be with you."

Finally he looks at her. "I'm not gonna be the reason you turn down an opportunity like Yates."

"You aren't the reason," Tessa tries to explain. "It's just—it's Sadie. She's making me choose between soccer and you." She feels tears well up in her eyes and wills herself not to cry. "I'm really confused right now. She's put me in a difficult position."

"Well," he crosses his arms, "I'll make it easy for you—I want to break up. It's better this way anyway—we're starting over next year, everything new. Being together would hold me back too."

"I don't want to start over," Tessa says. Tears spill over her cheeks, but she doesn't care anymore. "I don't want everything to be new. I want us to be together."

"But I'm telling you," Ben says. "It's over. We're done. I'm letting you go."

Tessa stands in shock as Ben walks away from her. This was not at all the way she imagined this day would go.

Ellen walks over to Tessa. "Hey," she says. "I'm sorry."

Tessa's voice catches. "This isn't what I want."

"Maybe not. But I think you have to let him go."

Tessa tries to catch her breath. She scrubs at her face before plopping herself on the ground, not caring at all about what it might do to Sadie's dress.

She expects Ben to tell them to get in the truck so they can leave already, but he just sits there. For a moment, Tessa wonders if he's changed his mind. She hears Ellen talking with him quietly. Finally, Ellen walks over to her.

"Ben said we can stay as long as you need."

"Of course," Tessa says, sniffling. "Because he's a good guy."

"He is," Ellen says. "He really is. I'm sorry. Sadie just doesn't know Ben."

"She doesn't know me," Tessa says. "I don't want to be in her sorority. I didn't want to break up with Ben just for her."

She and Ellen sit together by the side of the road in silence for a few more minutes before Tessa stands up and brushes herself off. She walks over to the truck, avoiding eye contact with Ben. Ellen climbs in the seat between them, and Tessa leans her head against the window. Every few minutes, she feels tempted to ask Ben to pull over so they can talk more, but something stops her every time.

***

The next few days are a blur for Tessa. She doesn't want to get out of bed, but if she misses classes or practice, she won't be able to play in the quarterfinals game.

She goes through the motions of sitting through her classes. She can't help herself from checking her phone every five minutes to see if Ben has called or texted.

Nothing.

Her eyes scan the hallways between classes, looking for him. Though their paths used to cross all the time at school, now they somehow manage to never run into each other.

She wonders if he's avoiding her.

That next Tuesday after school, Tessa sees a thick envelope with the Yates logo sitting on the kitchen table. Heart pounding, she drops her backpack and tears open the flap.

Dear Ms. Dobbs,

Congratulations! It is our pleasure . . .

Tessa reads the words. *Yowlers women's soccer team. Scholarship. Yates.* But all she can see in her mind is Sadie and the other Omega Phi girls sitting around the table, talking about things she doesn't care about. She sees Ben, standing off to the side of the road, willing to walk away from her. She sees Coach Miller, speaking in front of her players as if they're not even there.

Just days ago, Tessa would have been thrilled to receive this letter. Now, she doesn't know if she even wants to go to this school anymore.

Tessa changes into her workout clothes and heads into the barn. She shoots ball after ball into the net until her legs are exhausted.

She drops to the ground and stretches her legs in front of her, lazily passing the ball from one foot to the other. With each pass, a new question pops up in her head.

Does she want to join Sadie's sorority?

Does she want to be with Ben?

Does she want to play for the Yowlers?

Does she even want to go to Yates?

AN hour later, Tessa's phone buzzes with a call from an unknown number. She answers, having a feeling she knows who it is.

"Tessa," Coach Miller says when she picks up, "I have great news. I'm hoping you already received our letter in the mail?"

"I did."

"Excellent. We're very excited to make you an offer. I think you have great potential. With some hard work, I know we can whip you right into shape."

Tessa clenches her jaw at that. She takes a deep breath, knowing she's at least made one decision now.

"Coach Miller," she says, "thank you. This is a generous offer, and I think you're a great coach. But I don't think Yates is the right fit for me anymore."

"I see."

"I'm sorry to have to turn you down. Thank you again for giving me a chance."

There's a long pause on the other end. Tessa pulls her phone away from her head to check if Coach Miller hung up on her. But suddenly she hears the coach's voice again.

"Ms. Dobbs," she says.

"Yes?"

"The best athletes in the world not only work hard but have good instincts—instincts they can trust. I hope your instincts are right."

"Me too," Tessa says.

"Well," Coach Miller continues, "I'm sorry I won't be able to work you into the player I know you can be. But I'll be looking for you in the future, and I'll be cheering you on."

Tessa smiles and thanks her one last time. After they hang up, she wonders if she'll ever play on a field with fans in the stands cheering her on. This might have been her only chance, and she just let it go.

***

The Colts face the St. Theresa's Royals again in the quarterfinals game. Before the team goes out to the field, Tessa stands up on a bench.

"We've had a good season," she says to her teammates. "Today, all we can do is play with grit, play with heart, and play for the love of the game."

The girls cheer and clap. She continues, "If we lose, our season is done. And I want you all to know that, more than anything, I'd like to keep playing with all of you. You're incredible teammates. So let's do everything we can to pull out a win."

The girls throw their hands in the middle for one last cheer before they leave the locker room.

Ellen walks with Tessa as they head down to the field. "I told my sister what happened," she says. "About everything."

"What did she say?"

"She seemed disappointed, but she didn't say much actually." Ellen snorts. "Figures.

Sadie only looks out for herself." Then she stops and turns to Tessa. "I'm really sorry about everything. This is not what I wanted to happen."

"Don't be sorry," Tessa says. "You were just being a good friend, trying to help me out."

"But I didn't help. I messed everything up for you."

"No," Tessa says. "You didn't. There are other schools, and I'm going to be just fine."

***

When the game begins, Tessa feels more focused than she has ever before. Kellie Jones looks confident in the goal once again, and Tessa tries to match that confidence herself. She charges down the field, driving the ball ahead of her toward the Royals' goal.

She takes a shot and the ball barely skims the tips of Kellie's fingers. It flies just over the top of the net. The Carlton fans sigh in disappointment, but Tessa isn't worried. She can tell by the look in Kellie's eyes that that was a lucky save. She can feel that she'll have another shot against Kellie tonight.

In the second half, the score is 2–0 with the Royals in the lead. Kellie is on her game tonight, nothing is getting past her. Tessa grits her teeth as the minutes on the clock start, determined to get one—if not two—goals before the end of the game.

But no matter how many times she tries to take a shot, nothing goes in. Tessa rethinks her strategy, trying to pass to her teammates more and see if they have any better luck against Kellie.

With just minutes left, Ellen makes a shot that looks good. Tessa tenses up as she watches the ball sail through the air, only for it to be knocked out of the way by Kellie at the last moment.

"Nice try," Tessa says when Ellen jogs past her with an angry look on her face.

"I was so close!" Ellen groans. "That girl is good. One of us *has* to score on her."

When Ellen gets the ball next, two Royals players are closing in on her. Tessa races ahead and calls that she's open. Ellen shoots the ball her way. A Royals player tries to intercept the ball, but Tessa gets a hold of it first.

She moves toward the goal and time feels like it slows down. She raises her leg back and swings it forward. When her foot connects with the ball this time, she can feel that it's a good kick.

Kellie dives for it but the ball arcs just past her into a corner of the net. It's good!

The buzzer signaling the end of the game goes off.

Tessa finally gets her goal, and the game is over. It's the end of the season for the Carlton Colts. As far as Tessa knows, it could be the end of soccer for her altogether.

As Tessa heads off the field, her legs feeling as if they are made out of concrete, she hears someone calling after her. Kellie Jones jogs up to her.

"You're an incredible forward," she says. "The best I've ever seen."

"Thanks," Tessa says. "That means a lot."

"Are you playing anywhere next year?"

Tessa can't tell where she's going with this.

"Um, I don't have any plans yet. I was sort of talking with Yates for a while, but that didn't work out."

Kellie nods. "It's not quite official yet, but I'm planning to commit to play for Rushford-Moore University after I graduate," she explains. The look on Tessa's face must show that she's never heard of that school. "They're up north a few hours. Kind of a small school, but they revamped their women's soccer program a few years ago. Hired a new coach, made some good changes. I think they're gonna be a top team within the next few years."

"Oh," Tessa replies. "That's, uh, that's great."

Kellie smiles. "I'd love to have you on my team. I meant it when I said you're a great player—together, we could be unstoppable."

Tessa gapes at her.

"I think they still have an opening or two for next year. If you want, maybe I could put you in touch with the coach."

"Oh—that's—I don't even," Tessa stutters.

Kellie laughs and she joins in too. "That would be amazing. Thank you. But, I don't even know anything about this school."

"Well, look them up online. If you like what you see, why don't you text me and we can go from there." They exchange phone numbers, and Tessa promises to follow up with her.

"You better!" Kellie says with a playful smile. "I want you as my teammate in two years!"

MORE than a year later, Tessa comes home for winter break after her first semester at Rushford-Moore University. She's a benched player for her first year, but her coach thinks she shows a lot of promise and there are talks of her starting in next year's season. She managed to get a partial academic scholarship, and the school helped her with some financial aid too. Next year, she'll be eligible for an athletic scholarship.

Not only has the soccer team at Rushford-Moore worked out, but she loves the new friends she's made there. She and Ellen still stay in touch thanks to texting and social media. Her classes are challenging, and she finds herself trying new things all the time.

Sometimes, she can't believe how well it all turned out.

Back at home, she heads out into the barn, which isn't quite as empty as it used to be. Her parents got their farm certified organic and are finally making a profit. They brought in a small herd of cows again, and her father has gone back to farming full time. Tessa loves seeing her parents this happy and hopeful again.

Hay is stacked to the ceiling on one end of the loft. Before she came home, her dad made space up there for her to practice again. She works on her footwork for a bit and then starts taking some shots.

She's gathering up the soccer balls when she hears someone call her name. When she peers over the edge of the hayloft, she sees Ben standing there.

She and Ben hadn't talked for a while after their breakup. Tessa had a lot to focus on with the end of the soccer season and her new plans to go to Rushford-Moore. By the time everything had slowed down, she finally realized how angry she was that Ben had broken up with her just because he thought it would be "good for her." When she confronted him about it, they had an intense argument and didn't speak to each other for a long time again.

But over the summer, they ran into each other a few times and eventually got back on friendly terms. He got accepted to Yates and declared a major in engineering. He's met a few of her new friends through their occasional video chats, and they all get along with him easily.

"Need a goalie?" he asks, leaning one hand on the ladder.

She looks down at him and smiles. "Sure. But first, I want to hear how you've been."

They sit down on a hay bale and catch up. She doesn't know what might happen between her and Ben, or what else might change for her. But it's nice to know she has options.

ABOUT THE AUTHOR

K. R. Coleman is a teacher at the Loft Literary Center in Minneapolis, Minnesota. Recently, she was awarded a Minnesota State Arts Board Grant and Sustainable Artist Grant. She lives in Minneapolis with her husband, two boys, and two dogs named Happy and Gilmore.